rary

SPL

KT-419-883

C333778358

Note to parents, carers and teachers

Read it yourself is a series of modern stories, favourite characters and traditional tales written in a simple way for children who are learning to read. The books can be read independently or as part of a guided reading session.

Each book is carefully structured to include many high-frequency words vital for first reading. The sentences on each page are supported closely by pictures to help with understanding, and to offer lively details to talk about.

The books are graded into four levels that progressively introduce wider vocabulary and longer stories as a reader's ability and confidence grows.

Ideas for use

- Begin by looking through the book and talking about the pictures. Has your child heard this story before?

- Help your child with any words he does not know, either by helping him to sound them out or supplying them yourself.

- Developing readers can be concentrating so hard on the words that they sometimes don't fully grasp the meaning of what they're reading. Answering the puzzle questions at the end of the book will help with understanding.

For more information and advice on Read it yourself and book banding, visit **www.ladybird.com/readityourself**

Book Band 7

Level 2 is ideal for children who have received some reading instruction and can read short, simple sentences with help.

Special features:

Frequent repetition of main story words and phrases

Short, simple sentences

"Thanks for your help, everyone!" said Nutkin.

"That's what friends are for!" said Peter.

28 29

Large, clear type

Just then, Old Brown swooped down from the sky!

"You can't get away, Squirrel Nutkin," he called. "Everyone, get down here!" said Lily.

Careful match between story and pictures

14 15

Educational Consultant: Geraldine Taylor
Book Banding Consultant: Kate Ruttle

LADYBIRD BOOKS

UK | USA | Canada | Ireland | Australia
India | New Zealand | South Africa

Ladybird Books is part of the Penguin Random House group of companies
whose addresses can be found at global.penguinrandomhouse.com.

ladybird.com

Penguin
Random House
UK

Text adapted from Peter Saves the Day, first published by Puffin Books, 2014.
This version first published by Ladybird Books, 2015.
001

Ladybird, Read it yourself and the Ladybird logo are registered or
unregistered trademarks owned by Ladybird Books Ltd
Peter Rabbit TV series imagery and text © Frederick Warne & Co. Ltd &
Silvergate PPL Ltd, 2014
Layout and design © Frederick Warne & Co. Ltd, 2015
The 'Peter Rabbit' TV series is based on the works of Beatrix Potter.
Peter Rabbit™ & Beatrix Potter™ Frederick Warne & Co.
Frederick Warne & Co is the owner of all rights, copyrights and trademarks
in the Beatrix Potter character names and illustrations
Text adapted by Ellen Philpott

Printed in China

A CIP catalogue record for this book is available from the British Library

ISBN: 978-0-723-29528-0

The Angry Owl

Based on the Peter Rabbit™
TV series

Old Brown was chasing
Squirrel Nutkin all over
the woods.

"Help!" called Nutkin.

"Come in here!" said
Peter Rabbit. "What is
Old Brown chasing you for?"

"I took his glasses," said
Nutkin, "and now I can't
find them!"

"We will help you find them," said Lily.

"Thanks, everyone," said Nutkin.

"Come on, let's go!" said Peter. The friends ran into the woods.

"Where could the glasses be?" said Peter.

"Let's ask Jeremy Fisher," said Lily.

But Jeremy Fisher had not seen them.

Just then, Old Brown swooped down from the sky!

"You can't get away, Squirrel Nutkin," he called.

"Everyone, get down here!" said Lily.

"Now!" said Peter, and the friends all ran away.

Old Brown chased after them, but he could not get in.

"Come here, Squirrel Nutkin!" he called.

"Where could the glasses be?" said Peter.

"Let's ask Mrs Tiggy-Winkle," said Benjamin.

But Mrs Tiggy-Winkle had not seen them.

"No. That Nutkin just left berry stains!" she said.

19

Just then, Old Brown
swooped down from the sky.

"There you are," he called.
He chased Nutkin into
the woods.

"Where could the glasses be?" said Peter.

"Nutkin left berry stains," said Lily.

"The berry trees!" said Benjamin.

The rabbits ran to the berry trees.

"The glasses! There they are!" said Peter.

Peter took his friends to find Nutkin. Old Brown was swooping down on the squirrel.

"I will get you!" he said.

"Over here!" called Peter. "Come and get your glasses."

Just then, Peter let the glasses go.

"No!" called Old Brown. He chased after his glasses. Then he swooped away into the trees.

"Thanks for your help, everyone!" said Nutkin.

"That's what friends are for!" said Peter.

How much do you remember about the story of Peter Rabbit: The Angry Owl? Answer these questions and find out!

- Who is chasing Nutkin in the woods?

- What has Nutkin lost?

- Who do Peter and his friends speak to first?

- What does Nutkin leave at Mrs Tiggy-Winkle's house?

Look at the pictures and match them to the story words.

Peter

Benjamin

Old Brown

Lily

Squirrel Nutkin

glasses

Tick the books you've read!

Level 2

Level 3

Available on the App Store

ANDROID APP ON Google play

The Read it yourself with Ladybird app is now available